The Ugly Duckling

Parragon
Bath • New York • Cologne • Melbourne • Delhi
Hong Kong • Shenzhen • Singapore

Four steps for enjoyable reading

Traditional stories and fairy tales are a great way to begin reading practice. The stories and characters are familiar and lively. Follow the steps below to help your child become a confident and independent reader:

Step 1
Read the story aloud to your child. Run your finger under the words as you read.

Step 2
Look at the pictures and talk about what is happening.

Step 3
Read the simple text on the right-hand page together. When reading, some words come up again and again, such as **the**, **to**, **and**. Your child will quickly get to recognize these high-frequency words by sight.

Step 4
When your child is ready, encourage them to read the simple lines on their own.

One day, six fluffy yellow ducklings hatched from their eggs. Mother Duck was very happy.

"Cheep, cheep!" the ducklings called to their mother.

There was one big egg left in the nest.

At last, the big egg cracked open. Out popped a funny gray duckling with big black feet and a big black beak. The other ducks crowded around to look with Mother Duck.

"It does not look like a duckling," they said.

Mother Duck gathered up her fluffy yellow ducklings and her funny gray duckling.

"Follow me," she said. She led them through the farmyard. All the animals stopped to stare at the funny gray duckling.

The animals made fun of him.

When they got to the pond, Mother Duck and the little ducklings all swam off. The funny gray duckling was left behind.

"Go away," said the goose. "You are ugly."

“You are not one of us,”
she said.

The funny gray duckling went back to the barn. But the fluffy yellow ducklings wouldn't play with him.

"Go away," they said. "You are not like us. You don't belong here."

The little duckling was very sad.
He ran away.

The funny gray duckling walked for miles until he came to a cottage. A little old woman gave him some grain and milk.

"Go away," said the hen, "you are eating all my grain."

"Go away," said the cat, "you are drinking all my milk."

"And don't come back," said the cat and the hen.

The funny gray duckling went back to the pond. But winter was coming, and the pond was turning to ice.

The funny gray duckling was cold and hungry. He saw some fine swans fly over the pond.

"I wish I could fly up in the sky with the swans," he thought.

The swans did not see him. They flew far away.

At last, the winter turned to spring. The ducklings came back down to the pond. But they had grown up. Now they were ducks. They saw the ugly gray duckling. But he had grown up, too. He was not a duck at all.

"If I am not a duck, what am I?" he asked.

Then he looked down into the water and saw his reflection.

"I look just like a fine swan!" he said, surprised.

"I am a swan!" he shouted with joy.

Just then, the fine swans flew over and landed next to him on the pond.

"Hello," said one of the swans. "Do you want to come with us?"

He was so happy!

Now he could fly away with the other swans.